EARTHLETS
as explained by
Professor Xargle

PUFFIN UNICORN BOOKS

Published by the Penguin Group
Penguin Books USA Inc., 375 Hudson Street,
New York, New York 10014, U.S.A.
Penguin Books Ltd, 27 Wrights Lane, London W8 5TZ, England
Penguin Books Australia Ltd, Ringwood, Victoria, Australia
Penguin Books Canada Ltd, 10 Alcorn Avenue,
Toronto, Ontario, Canada M4V 3B2
Penguin Books (N.Z.) Ltd, 182-190 Wairau Road,
Auckland 10, New Zealand
Penguin Books Ltd, Registered Offices:
Harmondsworth, Middlesex, England

Library of Congress number 88-23692
ISBN 0-14-055293-6

Published in the United States by
Dutton Children's Books,
a division of Penguin Books USA Inc.
Printed in Hong Kong
First Puffin Unicorn Edition 1994
3 5 7 9 10 8 6 4 2

EARTHLETS, AS EXPLAINED BY PROFESSOR XARGLE is
also available in hardcover from Dutton Children's Books.

EARTHLETS
as explained by
Professor Xargle

by Jeanne Willis
illustrated by Tony Ross

A PUFFIN UNICORN

Good morning, class.

Today we are going to learn about Earthlets.

Earthlets come in different colors: pink, brown,
black and yellow, but not green.

They have one head but only two eyes. And they have two short tentacles and two longer ones, with feelers on the ends.

They use their feelers to help them catch wild animals called Fluffy and Kitty.

Earthlets grow fur on their heads, but not enough to keep them warm.

So they are wrapped in the fuzz of sheep.

Earthlings called Grandmas unravel the fuzz.
Then with two pointed sticks, they make it into
Earthlet wrappers.

Earthlets are born without fangs. At first, they drink only milk, through a hole in their faces called a mouth.

When they finish the milk, they are patted and squeezed so they won't explode.

After an Earthlet grows fangs, the parent Earthling sometimes takes a banana or the egg of a hen and mashes it with a shiny tool.

The mash is put on a little shovel and tipped into the
Earthlet's mouth, nose and ears.

Earthlets often leak. When they do, their bottom
tentacles are raised so the Earthlet can be pinned
into a white cloth or sealed in soft paper with tape.

During the day, Earthlets collect dirt, Fluffy hair, milk, and banana-mash.

Then they are placed in a plastic capsule with warm
water and a floating bird.

After soaking, they must be dried carefully so they won't shrink. Then they are sprinkled with dust so they won't stick to things.

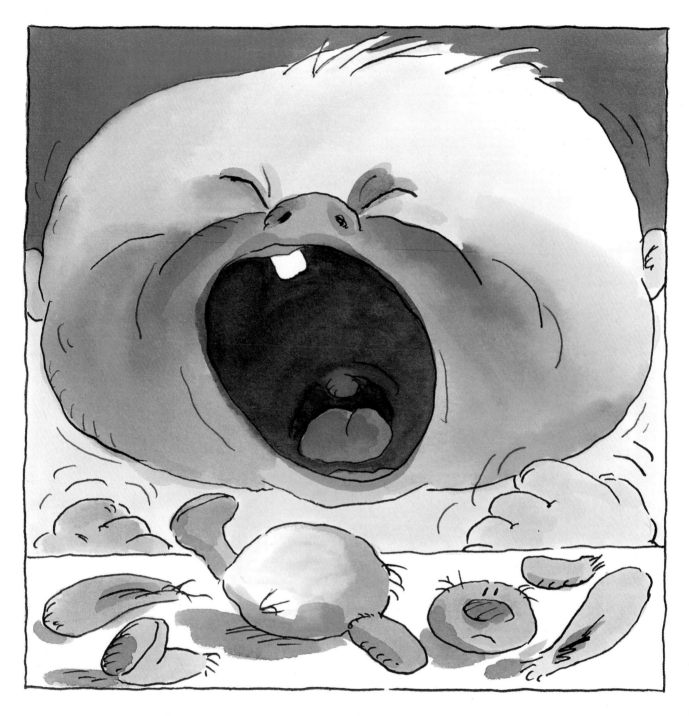

An Earthlet can be recognized by its roar:
"WAAAAAAAH!"

To quiet the Earthlet, the father Earthling flings it
into the atmosphere.

But he never ever drops it.

If the Earthlet keeps roaring, its mother pulls its feelers and says "This little piggy went to market" until the Earthlet makes *hee hee* noises.

At night the Earthlet goes to a place called beddy-
bye.

This is a rocking box that is soft inside. A small bear called Teddy lives there.

That is the end of today's lesson.

Now let's all put on our disguises and go see some
real Earthlets.

The spaceship leaves for planet Earth in five minutes.